The Boys
from
Baraboo

The Story
of the
Ringling Brothers

The Boys from Baraboo

an illustrated book for children of all ages

by

Barbara Harnack & Michael Lancaster

Published by
Ballyhoo Publishing

First Edition November 10, 2013
(Preview Edition May 19, 2013)

ISBN-978-0-578-12306-6

Written by Michael Lancaster
Illustrated by Barbara Harnack
Set design & photography by Michael Lancaster

A portion of the proceeds from sales of the book will be donated to animal welfare organizations. To find out what organizations are being supported visit www.RinglingBook.com

Printed in the USA
Signature Book Printing
www.sbpbooks.com

A long time ago in America there was a large family that lived in a little house. The Papa made leather harnesses for horses and wagons.

One day a man hired the Papa to make harnesses for a riverboat circus that was coming to their little town of McGregor, Iowa. He paid Papa with tickets to the circus. Papa and the oldest boys went to work right away because the show was coming the very next day.

The next morning the children heard the steam whistle sound of a calliope coming from a river boat.

The sound of music made from whistling steam was so exciting that everyone ran to the river to greet the riverboat circus.

When the family arrived at the river, they saw clowns, acrobats and jugglers, and strange and exotic animals. The circus performers off-loaded from the boat and made a parade. They went to a big field and set up a large tent called a *Big Top*.

Some of the brothers helped raise the tent and some watched and learned. That day they saw their first circus. It was the most fun they ever had!

The whole family sat together. They cheered and clapped and laughed and their lives changed forever.

A man walked
high overhead
on a tightrope.

And clowns
performed and
made everyone
laugh.

A woman swung high above on a trapeze and twirled and spun round and round.

Then dogs performed tricks and danced.

When it was over, and they were back at home, the family sat at the kitchen table and talked about what they had seen at the circus. Then finally, Johnny, the youngest said, "Let's make a circus of our own!" Everyone laughed with excitement, and Mama and Papa said they would help.

The whole family joined in the fun and they made a little circus show in the barn. Families from all over town came and gave them pennies to see their little show.

They took all of the money they made from the *One Penny Circus* and bought some canvas to make a tent. They gave a circus parade and people from all over town followed them to the family farm.

The whole family helped make the tent.

This time they charged five cents and they had more acts and made a bigger show. They saved their money so that one day they could make an even larger circus.

As the children grew up, Papa and Mama moved the whole family to Baraboo, Wisconsin, where Papa could have more work making harnesses for horses and wagons.

The boys went out to small towns in Wisconsin and made a concert and comedy company. They gave shows at village playhouses and town halls, where they played music, told jokes and danced and juggled.

One summer, the oldest brother named Al went to work for a circus, so he could learn how to make a real circus and teach his younger brothers. When he came home he had married a snake charmer named Louise. She was very beautiful and could also perform acts riding horses and was called an equestrian.

The boys took all their money and bought canvas to make a real circus tent. They joined together with eight other actors to make their first circus.

They partnered with an old circus man named Yankee Robinson and hired 9 farm boys to help drive 10 wagons, and in May of 1884 they went out to small towns in Wisconsin and Iowa to give their first circus performances.

They saved all their money and put it back
into their circus.

It grew so big that they had to travel
on railroad cars.

The *Ringling Brothers World's Greatest Show* grew faster and bigger than any other circus in the world. The owner's of other circuses asked them "Why is your circus growing so big?" And they told them, "It's because we have rules, like being honest and fair, telling the truth, and we treat animals with respect."

The Boys from Baraboo bought the next biggest circus in the world. It was called *The Greatest Show on Earth.* When they put the two great shows together they had the largest and best show in the world!

And it all started
with a dream!

AL

OTTO

ALF T.

CHARLEY

JOHN

Acknowledgements

This project could never have been completed had we tried to accomplish it on our own. Many people and institutions contributed, either directly or by inspiration. The story of the Ringling Brothers easily wrote itself, as we merely distilled what we thought were the [important] parts from history, and by adding a point of view made it palatable, for children. This was not difficult as the Ringlings started their venture as children.

First of all we must acknowledge the five original Ringling Brothers for their foresight and willingness to be dreamers and then act upon their dreams. Good credit must be given to the entire family from Mama and Papa to brothers Gus and Henry, (often not credited because they were not the original five brothers), and of course sister Ida, whom in early years was present sewing tents and uniforms. Thank you Jayne Shatz, for after learning of Michael's novel, suggested we create a book to tell the Ringling story to children. We owe a special thank you to Talina Melenchenko for loaning and helping us find miniature props of all different scales to help bring the scenes to life. Thank you to the Warren and Doubrava family for searching deep into crates and finding Uncle John's trains in order to construct a train scene, and of course posthumously to Uncle John, for building such train scenes himself, in the twilight of his life. Thank you Melinda Bon'ewell for loaning your miniature houses. Thanks to Betty Warren, Michael's mother, for walking on Bayshore Road and peering down the long drive to the great Ringling properties and asking, "Who are these people?" Michael would not have been born if Betty had not asked that question. Thanks to the Ringling Museum for its many exhibits, including The Tibbals Learning Center and the wonderful models built by Howard Tibbals, and to Circus World Museum, in Baraboo, WI, for keeping the original 'Ringlingville' alive.

Finally, Barbara and I wish to thank each other for the spirit of collaboration and being dreamers and doers. This was the Ringling way, for it is not enough to just dream and do nothing, any more than it is to be just a doer and not follow a dream. This story is for dreamers, and we hope, in Ringling fashion, it will awaken your dreams and you will be inspired to make them become real. In each of us - no matter what age, there is a child, fresh and new to the world, so, this book is for you, "Ladies and Gentleman, Children of all ages..."

Barbara Harnack & Michael Lancaster

Barbara Harnack & Michael Lancaster

Harnack & Lancaster joined forces in the studio in 1980, after five years in relationship, while Barbara Harnack finished her education at Parsons School of Design with an emphasis on 3-D illustration, Michael Lancaster was completing an apprenticeship at The Red Rock Pottery, in Hillsdale, NY. The couple have worked together both individually and collaboratively in ceramics for over thirty years. During this time Lancaster talked extensively about writing a novel on his ancestors, The Ringling Brothers, which he published in 2012. That year they began a dialogue about telling the story for children. Using her background in illustration, Harnack came up with the idea of hand sculpting every character and using them to tell the story. This technique was also inspired by the young Ringling boys who gave performances and told stories in their barn, using miniature sets and hand painted scenes, in the 1870's. Each character has been studied and sculpted by Barbara Harnack. The initial story was written by Michael Lancaster and then the couple devised and designed each scene. Then each scene was built in a light box by Lancaster and photographed. Attention has been given to historic detail and accuracy of harnesses and even circus logistics and rigging, without losing the freedom of illustration. The desired effect was to give the reader and audience a feeling of 'being there', without loosing the wonder of toys and illustration. This story is an artwork in itself and is designed for "children of all ages." It is meant to return the audience to a simpler time, the Golden Age of Circus, of childhood innocence, grass roots values, and the pursuit of making a dream come true. A percentage of the proceeds of sales of the book will be donated to animal welfare groups. For more information on this and on other books by Barbara Harnack and Michael Lancaster visit www.RinglingBook.com.

Awarded an "Honorable Mention" by
The Purple Dragonfly Book Awards - 2013
for "Picture Books 6yrs and up."

A Purple Dragonfly award tells parents they're giving
their children the very best in reading excellence...

Learn more at www.FiveStarBookAwards.com